AN EVENINGS ENTERTAINMENT
-FANTASY AND HORROR CLASSICS-

BY

M. R. JAMES

British Library Cataloguing-in-Publication Data
A catalogue record for this book is available from the
British Library

M. R. JAMES

Montague Rhodes James was born in Kent, England in 1862. An intellectually gifted child, he excelled academically at both Temple Grove School and Eton College before enrolling at King's College, Cambridge. A highly respected scholar to this day, James' areas of research interest were apocryphal Biblical literature and mediaeval illuminated manuscripts. He was, by turns, Fellow, Dean, and Tutor at King's College, and in 1905 was installed as Provost. James was a highly sociable man, and he travelled widely throughout Europe.

James came to writing fiction relatively late, not publishing his first collection of short stories – Ghost Stories of an Antiquary (1904) – until the age of 42. Many of his tales were written as Christmas Eve entertainments and read aloud to friends. James described his introduction to ghosts in 1931: "In my childhood I chanced to see a toy Punch and Judy set, with figures cut out in cardboard. One of these was The Ghost. It was a tall figure habited in white with an unnaturally long and narrow head, also surrounded with white, and a dismal visage. Upon this my conceptions of a ghost were based, and for years it permeated my dreams." James believed that must a good story must "put the reader into the position of saying to himself: 'If I'm not careful, something of this kind may happen to me!'" He eventually published five collections of his ghost stories, all of which were reprinted and adapted numerous times.

Modern scholars now see James as having redefined the ghost story for the 20th century by abandoning many of the formal Gothic clichés of his predecessors and using more realistic contemporary settings. However, James's tales tend to reflect his own antiquarian interests, and he is seen as the founder of the 'antiquarian ghost story'. His first two collections – Ghost Stories of an Antiquary (1904) and More Ghost Stories (1911) – are generally regarded as his most important, containing as they do the well-known stories 'Number 13', 'Count Magnus', 'Oh, Whistle and I'll Come to You, My Lad' and 'Casting the Runes'.

The onset of World War One marked the beginning of the end of James' golden years in Cambridge. In 1918, he accepted the post of Provost of Eton College. He was awarded the Order of Merit in 1930, and died in 1936, aged 73.

AN EVENINGS ENTERTAINMENT

Nothing is more common form in old-fashioned books than the description of the winter fireside, where the aged grandam narrates to the circle of children that hangs on her lips story after story of ghosts and fairies, and inspires her audience with a pleasing terror. But we are never allowed to know what the stories were. We hear, indeed, of sheeted spectres with saucer eyes, and—still more intriguing—of 'Rawhead and Bloody Bones' (an expression which the Oxford Dictionary traces back to 1550), but the context of these striking images eludes us.

Here, then, is a problem which has long obsessed me; but I see no means of solving it finally. The aged grandams are gone, and the collectors of folk-lore began their work in England too late to save most of the actual stories which the grandams told. Yet such things do not easily die quite out, and imagination, working on scattered hints, may be able to devise a picture of an evening's entertainment, such an one as Mrs. Marcet's Evening Conversations, Mr. Joyce's Dialogues on Chemistry and somebody else's Philosophy in Sport made Science in Earnest aimed at extinguishing by substituting for Error and Superstition the light of Utility and Truth; in some such terms as these:

Charles: I think, papa, that 1 now understand the properties of the lever, which you so kindly explained to me on Saturday; but I have been very much puzzled since then in thinking about the pendulum, and have wondered why it is that, when you stop it, the clock does not go on any more.

Papa: (You young sinner, have you been meddling with the clock in the hall? Come here to me! No, this must be a gloss that has somehow crept into the text.) Well, my boy, though I do not wholly approve of your conducting without my supervision experiments which may possibly impair the usefulness of a valuable scientific instrument, I will do my best to explain the principles of the pendulum to you. Fetch me a piece of stout whipcord from the drawer in my study, and ask cook to be so good as to lend you one of the weights which she uses in her kitchen.

And so we are off.

How different the scene in a household to which the beams of Science have not yet penetrated! The Squire, exhausted by a long day after the partridges, and replete with food and drink, is snoring on one side of the fireplace. His old mother sits opposite to him knitting, and the children (Charles and Fanny, not Harry and Lucy: they would never have stood it) are gathered about her knee.

Grandmother: Now, my dears, you must be very good and quiet, or you'll wake your father, and you know what'll happen then.

Charles: Yes, I know: he'll be woundy cross-tempered

and send us off to bed.

Grandmother (stops knitting and speaks with severity): What's that? Fie upon you, Charles! that's not a way to speak. Now I was going to have told you a story, but if you use such-like words, I shan't. (Suppressed outcry: 'Oh, granny!') Hush! hush! Now I believe you have woke your father!

Squire (thickly): Look here, mother, if you can't keep them brats quiet

Grandmother: Yes, John, yes! it's too bad. I've been telling them if it happens again, off to bed they shall go.

Squire relapses.

Grandmother: There, now, you see, children, what did I tell you? you must be good and sit still. And I'll tell you what: tomorrow you shall go a-blackberrying, and if you bring home a nice basketful, I'll make you some jam.

Charles: Oh yes, granny, do! and I know where the best blackberries are: I saw 'em today.

Grandmother: And where's that, Charles?

Charles: Why, in the little lane that goes up past Collins's cottage. Grandmother (laying down her knitting): Charles! whatever you do, don't you dare to pick one single blackberry in that lane. Don't you know—but there, how should you—what was I thinking of? Well, anyway, you mind what I say

Charles and Fanny: But why, granny? Why shouldn't we pick 'em there?

Grandmother: Hush! hush! Very well then, I'll tell you

7

all about it, only you mustn't interrupt. Now let me see. When I was quite a little girl that lane had a bad name, though it seems people don't remember about it now. And one day—dear me, just as it might be tonight—I told my poor mother when I came home to my supper—a summer evening it was—I told her where I'd been for my walk, and how I'd come back down that lane, and I asked her how it was that there were currant and gooseberry bushes growing in a little patch at the top of the lane. And oh, dear me, such a taking as she was in! She shook me and she slapped me, and says she, 'You naughty, naughty child, haven't I forbid you twenty times over to set foot in that lane? and here you go dawdling down it at night-time,' and so forth, and when she'd finished I was lonely place like that in the middle of the night.' And Mr. Davis smiled, and the young man, who'd been listening, said, 'Oh, we don't want for company at such times,' and my father said he couldn't help thinking Mr. Davis made some kind of sign, and the young man went on quick, as if to mend his words, and said, 'That's to say, Mr. Davis and me's company enough for each other, ain't we, master? and then there's a beautiful air there of a summer night, and you can see all the country round under the moon, and it looks so different, seemingly, to what it do in the daytime. Why, all them harrows on the down -'

And then Mr. Davis cut in, seeming to be out of temper with the lad, and said, 'Ah yes, they're old-fashioned places, ain't they, sir? Now, what would you think was the purpose of them?' And my father said (now, dear me, it seems funny, doesn't it, that I should recollect all this: but it took my fancy at the time, and though it's dull perhaps for you, I can't help finishing it out now), well, he said, 'Why, I've heard, Mr. Davis, that they're all graves, and I know, when I've had occasion to plough up one, there's always been some old bones and pots turned up. But whose graves they are, I don't know: people say the ancient Romans were all about this country at one time, but whether they buried their people like that I can't tell.' And Mr. Davis shook his head, thinking, and said, 'Ah, to be sure: well they look to me to be older-like than the ancient Romans, and dressed different - that's to say, according to the pictures the Romans was in armour, and you didn't never find no armour, did you, sir, by what you said?' And my father was rather surprised and said, 'I don't know that I mentioned anything about armour, but it's true I don't remember to have found any. But you talk as if you'd seen 'em, Mr. Davis,' and they both of them laughed, Mr. Davis and the young man, and Mr. Davis said, 'Seen 'em, sir? that would be a difficult matter after all these years. Not but what I should like well enough to know more about them old times and people, and what they worshipped and all.' And my father said, 'Worshipped? Well, I dare say they worshipped the old man on the hill.' 'Ah, indeed!' Mr. Davis said, 'well, I shouldn't wonder,' and my father went on and told them what he'd heard and read about the heathens and their sacrifices: what you'll learn some day for yourself, Charles, when you go to school and begin your Latin. And they seemed to be very much interested, both of them; but my father said he couldn't help thinking the most of what he was saying was no news to them. That was the only time he ever had much talk with Mr. Davis, and it stuck in his mind, particularly, he said, the young man's word about not wanting for company: because in those days there was a lot of talk in the villages round about - why, but for my father interfering, the almost too much taken aback to say anything: but I did make her believe that was the first I'd ever heard of it; and that was no more than the truth. And then, to be sure, she was sorry she'd been so short with me, and to make up she told me the whole story after my supper. And since then I've often heard the same from the old people in the place, and had my own reasons besides for thinking there was something in it.

Now, up at the far end of that lane - let me see, is it on the right or the left-hand side as you go up? - the left-hand side - you'll find a little patch of bushes and rough ground in the field, and something like a broken old hedge round about, and you'll notice there's some old gooseberry and currant bushes growing among it - or there used to be, for it's years now since I've been up that way. Well, that means there was a cottage stood there, of course; and in that cottage, before I was born or thought of, there lived a man named Davis. I've heard that he wasn't born in the parish, and it's true there's nobody of that name been living about here since I've known the place. But however that may be, this Mr. Davis lived very much to himself and very seldom went to the public-house, and he didn't work for any of the farmers, having as it seemed enough money of his own to get along. But he'd go to the town on market-days and take up his letters at the post-house where the mails called. And one day he came back from market, and brought a young man with him; and this young man and he lived together for some long time, and went about together, and whether he just did the work of the house for Mr. Davis, or whether Mr. Davis was his teacher in some way, nobody seemed to know. I've heard he was a pale, ugly young fellow and hadn't much to say for himself. Well, now, what did those two men do with themselves? Of course I can't tell you half the foolish things that the people got into their heads, and we know, don't we, that you mustn't speak evil when you aren't sure it's true, even when people are dead and gone. But as I said, those two were always about together, late and early, up on the downland and below in the woods: and there was one walk in particular that they'd take regularly once a month, to the place where you've seen that old figure cut out in the hill-side; and it was noticed that in the summer time when they took that walk, they'd camp out all night, either there or somewhere near by. I remember once my father - that's your great-grandfather -told me he had spoken to Mr. Davis about it (for it's his land he lived on) and asked him why he was so fond of going there, but he only said: 'Oh, it's a wonderful old place, sir, and I've always been fond of the old-fashioned things, and when him (that was his man he meant) and me are together there, it seems to bring back the old times so plain.' And my father said, 'Well,' he said, 'it may suit you, but I shouldn't like a people here would have ducked an old lady for a witch.

Charles: What does that mean, granny, ducked an old lady for a witch? Are there witches here now?

Grandmother: No, no, dear! why, what ever made me stray off like that? No, no, that's quite another affair. What I was going to say was that the people in other places round about believed that some sort of meetings went on at night-time on that hill where the man is, and that those who went there were up to no good. But don't you interrupt me now, for it's getting late. Well, I suppose it was a matter of three years that Mr. Davis and this young man went on living together: and then all of a sudden, a dreadful thing happened. I don't know if I ought to tell you. (Outcries of 'Oh yes! yes, granny, you must,' etc.). Well, then, you must promise not to get frightened and go screaming out in the middle of the night. (No, no, we won't, of course not!') One morning very early towards the turn of the year, I think it was in September, one of the woodmen had to go up to his work at the top of the long covert just as it was getting light; and just where there were some few big oaks in a sort of clearing deep in the wood he saw at a distance a white thing that looked like a man through the mist, and he was in two minds about going on, but go on he did, and made out as he came near that it was a man, and more than that, it was Mr. Davis's young man: dressed in a sort of white gown he was, and hanging by his neck to the limb of the biggest oak, quite, quite dead: and near his feet there lay on the ground a hatchet all in a gore of blood. Well, what a terrible sight that was for anyone to come upon in that lonely place! This poor man was nearly out of his wits: he dropped everything he was carrying and ran as hard as ever he could straight down to the Parsonage, and woke them up and told what he'd seen. And old Mr. White, who was the parson then, sent him off to get two or three of the best men, the blacksmith and the churchwardens and what not, while he dressed himself, and all of them went up to this dreadful place with a horse to lay the poor body on and take it to the house. When they got there, everything was just as the woodman had said: but it was a terrible shock to them all to see how the corpse was dressed, specially to old Mr. White, for it seemed to him to be like a mockery of the church surplice that was on it, only, he told my father, not the same in the fashion of it. And when they came to take down the body from the oak

13

tree they found there was a chain of some metal round the neck and a little ornament like a wheel hanging to it on the front, and it was very old looking, they said. Now in the meantime they had sent off a boy to run to Mr. Davis's house and see whether he was at home; for of course they couldn't but have their suspicions. And Mr. White said they must send too to the constable of the next parish, and get a message to another magistrate (he was a magistrate himself), and so there was running hither and thither. But my father as it happened was away from home that night, otherwise they would have fetched him first. So then they laid the body across the horse, and they say it was all they could manage to keep the beast from bolting away from the time they were in sight of the tree, for it seemed to be mad with fright. However, they managed to bind the eyes and lead it down through the wood and back into the village street; and there, just by the big tree where the stocks are, they found a lot of the women gathered together, and this boy whom they'd sent to Mr. Davis's house lying in the middle, as white as paper, and not a word could they get out of him, good or bad. So they saw there was something worse yet to come, and they made the best of their way up the lane to Mr. Davis's house. And when they got near that, the horse they were leading seemed to go mad again with fear, and reared up and screamed, and struck out with its fore-feet and the man that was leading it was as near as possible being killed, and the dead body fell off its back. So Mr. White bid them get the horse away as quick as might be, and they carried the body straight into the living-room, for the door stood open. And then they saw what it was that had given the poor boy such a fright, and they guessed why the horse went mad, for you know horses can't bear the smell of dead blood.

There was a long table in the room, more than the length of a man, and on it there lay the body of Mr. Davis. The eyes were bound over with a linen band and the arms were tied across the back, and the feet were bound together with another band. But the fearful thing was that the breast being quite bare, the bone of it was split through from the top downwards with an axe! Oh, it was a terrible sight; not one there but turned faint and ill with it, and had to go out into the fresh air. Even Mr. White, who was what you might call a hard nature of a man, was quite overcome and said a prayer for strength in the garden.

At last they laid out the other body as best they could in the room, and searched about to see if they could find out how such a frightful thing had come to pass. And in the cupboards they found a quantity of herbs and jars with liquors, and it came out, when people that understood such matters had looked into it, that some of these liquors were drinks to put a person asleep. And they had little doubt that that wicked young man had put some of this into Mr. Davis's drink, and then used him as he did, and, after that, the sense of his sin had come upon him and he had cast himself away.

Well now, you couldn't understand all the law business that had to be done by the coroner and the magistrates; but there was a great coming and going of people over it for the next day or two, and then the people of the parish got together and agreed that they couldn't bear the thought of those two being buried in die churchyard alongside of Christian people; for I must tell you there were papers and writings found in the drawers and cupboards that Mr. White and some other clergymen looked into; and they put their names to a paper that said these men were guilty, by their own allowing, of the dreadful sin of idolatry; and they feared there were some in the neighbouring places that were not free from that wickedness, and called upon them to repent, lest the same fearful thing that was come to these men should befall them also; and then they burnt those writings. So then, Mr. White was of the same mind as the parishioners, and late one evening twelve men that were chosen went with him to that evil house, and with them they took two biers made very roughly for the purpose and two pieces of black cloth, and down at the cross-road, where you take the turn for Bascombe and Wilcombe, there were other men waiting with torches, and a pit dug, and a great crowd of people gathered together from all round about. And the men that went to the cottage went in with their hats on their heads, and four of them took the two bodies and laid them on the biers and covered them over with the black cloths, and no one said a word, but they bore them down the lane, and they were cast into the pit and covered over with stones and earth, and then Mr. White spoke to the people that were gathered together. My father was there, for he had come back when he heard the news, and he said he never should forget the strangeness of the sight, with the torches burning and those two black things huddled together in the pit, and not a sound from any of the people, except it might be a child or a woman whimpering with the fright. And so, when Mr. White had finished speaking, they all turned away and left them lying there.

They say horses don't like the spot even now, and I've heard there was something of a mist or a light hung about for a long time after, but I don't know the truth of that. But this I do know, that next day my father's business took him past the opening of the lane, and he saw three or four little knots of people standing at different places along it, seemingly in a state of mind about something; and he rode up to them, and asked what was the matter. And they ran up to him and said, 'Oh, Squire, it's the blood! Look at the blood!' and kept on like that. So he got off his horse and they showed him, and there, in four places, I think it was, he saw great patches in the road, of blood: but he could hardly see it was blood, for almost every spot of it was covered with great black flies, that never changed their place or moved. And that blood was what had fallen out of Mr. Davis's body as they bore it down the lane. Well, my father couldn't bear to do more than just take in the nasty sight so as to be sure of it, and then he said to one of those men that was there, 'Do you make haste and fetch a basket or a barrow full of clean earth out of the churchyard and spread it over these places, and I'll wait here till you come back.' And very soon he came back, and the old man that was sexton with him, with a shovel and the earth in a hand-barrow: and they set it down at the first of the places and made ready to cast the earth upon it; and as as ever they did that, what do you think? the flies that were on it rose up in the air in a kind of a solid cloud and moved off up the lane towards the house, and the sexton (he was parish clerk as well) stopped and looked at them and said to my father, 'Lord of flies, sir,' and no more would he say. And just the same it was at the other places, every one of them.

Charles: But what did he mean, granny?

Grandmother: Well, dear, you remember to ask Mr. Lucas when you go to him for your lesson tomorrow. I can't stop now to talk about it: it's long past bed-time for you already. The next thing was, my father made up his mind no one was going to live in that cottage again, or yet use any of the things that were in it: so, though it was one of the best in the place, he sent round word to the people that it was to be done away with, and anyone that wished could bring a faggot to the burning of it; and that's what was done. They built a pile of wood in the living-room and loosened the thatch so as the fire could take good hold, and then set it alight; and as there was no brick, only the chimney-stack and the oven, it wasn't long before it was all gone. I seem to remember seeing the chimney when I was a little girl, but that fell down of itself at last.

Now this that I've got to is the last bit of all. You may be sure that for a long time the people said Mr. Davis and that young man were seen about, the one of them in the wood and both of them where the house had been, or passing together down the lane, particularly in the spring of the year and at autumn-time. I can't speak to that, though if we were sure there are such things as ghosts, it would seem likely that people like that wouldn't rest quiet. But I can tell you this, that one evening in the month of March, just before your grandfather and I were married, we'd been taking a long walk in the woods together and picking flowers and talking as young people will that are courting; and so much taken up with each other that we never took any particular notice where we were going. And on a sudden I cried out, and your grandfather asked what was the matter. The matter was that I'd felt a sharp prick on the back of my hand, and I snatched it to me and saw a black thing on it, and struck it with the other hand and killed it. And I showed it him, and he was a man who took notice of all such things, and he said, 'Well, I've never seen ought like that fly before,' and though to my own eye it didn't seem very much out of the common, I've no doubt he was right.

And then we looked about us, and lo and behold if we weren't in the very lane, just in front of the place where that house had stood, and, as they told me after, just where the men set down the biers a minute when they bore them out of the garden gate. You may be sure we made haste away from there; at least, I made your grandfather come away quick, for I was wholly upset at finding myself there; but he would have lingered about out of curiosity if I'd have let him. Whether there was anything about there more than we could see I shall never be sure: perhaps it was partly the venom of that horrid fly's bite that was working in me that made me feel so strange; for, dear me, how that poor arm and hand of mine did swell up, to be sure! I'm afraid to tell you how large it was round! and the pain of it, too! Nothing my mother could put on it had any power over it at all, and it wasn't till she was persuaded by our old nurse to get the wise man over at Bascombe to come and look at it, that I got any peace at all. But he seemed to know all about it, and said I wasn't the first that had been taken that way. 'When the sun's gathering his strength,' he said, 'and when he's in the height of it, and when he's beginning to lose his hold, and when he's in his weakness, them that haunts about that lane had best to sake heed to themselves.' But what it was he bound on my arm and what he said over it, he wouldn't tell us. After that I soon got well again, but since then I've heard often enough of people suffering much the same as I did; only of late years it doesn't seem to happen but very seldom: and maybe things like that do die out in the course of time.

But that's the reason, Charles, why I say to you that I won't have you gathering me blackberries, no, nor eating them either, in that lane; and now you know all about it, I don't fancy you'll want to yourself. There! Off to bed you go this minute. What's that, Fanny? A light in your room? The idea of such a thing! You get yourself undressed at once and say your prayers, and perhaps if your father doesn't want me when he wakes up, I'll come and say good-night to you. And you, Charles, if I hear anything of you frightening your little sister on the way up to your bed, I shall tell your father that very moment, and you know what happened to you the last time.

The door closes, and granny, after listening intently for a minute or two, resumes her knitting. The Squire still slumbers.